P9-AET-168

Amelia Bedelia

Shapes Up

Amelia Bedelia

Shapes Up

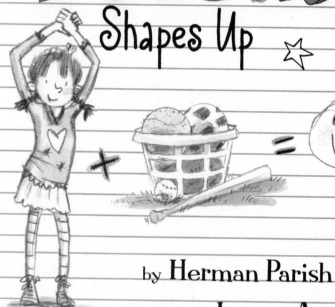

by Herman Parish

pictures by Lynne Avril

me

 Greenwillow Books

An Imprint of HarperCollins Publishers

Library of Congress Cataloging-in-Publication Data
Parish, Herman.
Amelia Bedelia shapes up / by Herman Parish ; pictures by Lynne Avril.
pages cm.—(Amelia Bedelia ; #5)
Summary: Picked last for kickball, Amelia Bedelia gets another chance to prove her athleticism
when her class holds a mini-Oylympics.
ISBN 978-0-06-233397-1 (hardback)—ISBN 978-0-06-233396-4 (pbk. ed.)—ISBN 978-0-06-233399-5 (pob)
[1. Sports—Fiction. 2. Schools—Fiction. 3. Humorous stories.] I. Avril, Lynne, (date) illustrator. II. Title.
PZ7.P2185Arbe 2014 [Fic]—dc23 2014008703

14 15 16 17 18 CG/RRDH 10 9 8 7 6 5 4 3 2 1 First Edition

 Greenwillow Books

For Skip Flanagan—

always in shape—H. P.

For Jim and Marybeth—L. A.

Contents

Chapter 1

Heads Up!

Amelia Bedelia did not wake up and say to herself, *Gee, what a beautiful day. I can't wait to look silly in front of all my friends.*

Amelia Bedelia would never wish that on anyone, much less herself. But that is exactly what happened. Doubly worse, it happened twice!

1

$$\frac{3}{4} = \frac{6}{8}$$

$$\frac{2}{8} = \frac{1}{4}$$

After doing fractions all morning, Amelia Bedelia and her friends were ready for recess. When Mrs. Robbins let them out early, they raced to the playground.

"Last one to the water fountain has to add up ten fractions, except Amelia Bedelia!" yelled Rose.

Rose was making an exception for Amelia Bedelia because Amelia Bedelia was the reason they had gotten out early for recess. She had given their math teacher,

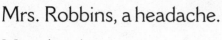

Mrs. Robbins, a headache. Here's why:

"Amelia Bedelia," said Mrs. Robbins at the beginning of math class, "what if I gave you a pie—"

"Thank you," said Amelia Bedelia. "I love pie."

"I'm not really giving you a pie," said Mrs. Robbins. "Just pretend."

"Okay," said Amelia Bedelia.

Mrs. Robbins continued, "Now suppose eight people want a piece."

"No problem," said Amelia Bedelia. "I'd cut it into eight equal pieces."

"That's correct," said Mrs. Robbins. "But what if you had served half the pie,

and then four more people showed up?"

"I'd bake them cupcakes," said Amelia Bedelia. "Pretend cupcakes."

"Pretend you can't bake," said Mrs. Robbins. "Stick with the pie. What fraction would the others get?"

$\frac{1}{3}$
$\frac{1}{3}$
$\frac{1}{3}$

"I've never tasted fraction pie," said Amelia Bedelia. "Is it good?

"A fraction isn't a flavor," said Mrs. Robbins. "It is a piece of the whole."

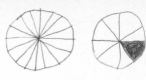

"But holes are empty," said Amelia Bedelia. "Am I serving pieces of nothing?"

"I mean the whole pie," said Mrs. Robbins. "I'll give you a hint. Half of the pie is gone, right? So you'd cut the other half into eight pieces—eight sixteenths, which is equal to four eighths, or two quarters."

"Then that's easy," said Amelia Bedelia. "If half a pie is just two quarters, I'd spend fifty cents and buy another half a pie for the new people."

"Pretend you don't have any cents," said Mrs. Robbins.

"I don't have to pretend that," said

$$\frac{8}{16} = \frac{4}{8} = \frac{2}{4} = \frac{1}{2}$$

5

$$\frac{8}{16} = \frac{1}{2}$$

$$\frac{8}{16} = \frac{4}{8} = \frac{2}{4} = \frac{1}{2}$$ $$\frac{8}{16} = \frac{1}{2}$$

Amelia Bedelia. "Sharing one puny pie with twelve people makes no sense at all."

The other kids had been trying not to laugh all along, but now they laughed out

loud. Mrs. Robbins was not laughing. She was rubbing her forehead.

"Pretend you know everything there is to know about fractions," Mrs. Robbins said with a sigh. "We'll try this again tomorrow. I think we all deserve an early recess."

This was too good to be true. No one moved a muscle until Mrs. Robbins added, "I'm not pretending!"

Amelia Bedelia and her friends took turns drinking from the water fountain. Then Rose and Dawn picked teams for a game of kickball. One after another, girls joined Rose or Dawn on the field until only Amelia Bedelia was left.

It was Dawn's turn, and Amelia Bedelia began jogging toward her.

"I choose the water fountain," said Dawn.

Amelia Bedelia stopped in her tracks. The other girls burst out laughing.

"That's mean," said Rose. "You have to pick Amelia Bedelia."

"Why?" asked Dawn. "She makes mistakes. Last time, we lost because of her. At least a water fountain won't goof up."

"I'll tell you why," said Rose. "If the water fountain is on your team, then my team can't get a drink without your permission. The water

8

fountain is for everybody.
That's why Amelia Bedelia
is for you."

Amelia Bedelia's cheeks
were getting redder and
redder. She had never felt so embarrassed
in her entire life. How could she come
in second place to a rusty, leaky water
fountain? Weren't they all friends? Had
Dawn forgotten that she had feelings?

Dawn just shook her head. Then she
motioned for Amelia Bedelia to come
over and join her. Amelia Bedelia felt like
running the other way, running all the
way home. Instead
she nodded, put a
smile on her face,

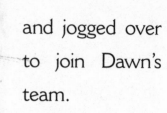

and jogged over to join Dawn's team.

Dawn put Amelia Bedelia in the outfield— the way, *way* out outfield. Amelia Bedelia stood there by herself for the entire game. But right before recess ended, Holly kicked the ball with all her might. It soared up, up, up in a high arc until it was a tiny dot, like a period at the end of a sentence. Then it began falling down, down, down toward Amelia Bedelia.

"Catch it!" hollered Dawn from the pitcher's mound. "Catch it and we win!"

Amelia Bedelia put her arms up and ran toward where she thought the ball would land. The sun was right in her eyes. She had to remind herself that it was just a red bouncy ball she was hoping to catch, and not a fiery asteroid screaming toward earth. She could do it. She could catch it! But it hurt to look into the sun and try to see the ball. Her eyes were watering. Amelia Bedelia blinked, glancing at the ground for just a second. She glimpsed Holly rounding second base on her way home with the winning run. . . .

BO-INNNNG! The ball hit the top of Amelia Bedelia's head so hard it knocked her on her butt. The ball bounced back up in the air. Penny made a diving catch,

right before the ball hit the ground. Holly was out. Game over. They'd won!

Everyone ran to Amelia Bedelia to make sure she was all right. Dawn helped her up while Penny brushed the dirt and grass off her back.

"Awesome teamwork!" said Dawn. "Amelia Bedelia, you can be on my side any day."

Yay!

Chapter 2

Water ~~Boy~~ Girl

When Amelia Bedelia got home from school, Dawn's remark about the water fountain was still bothering her. How dare Dawn pick a crummy water fountain for her team before picking her? Dawn was her friend! It

6 × 2 knees = double ouch!

reminded Amelia Bedelia of the time she had skinned both her knees at the beach and then went swimming. The salt water had really stung! Only now her feelings were hurting, not her knees.

After Amelia Bedelia set the table for dinner, she went outside and sat on the front steps. Her dog, Finally, sat down next to her and put her paw on her knee. Amelia Bedelia scratched Finally's furry ears. They waited for her father to come home from work. He always had some joke or said something wacky. Her

dad could always cheer her up.

She did not have to wait long. As he was turning off the sidewalk and onto their front walk, he bellowed loud enough for the neighbors to hear, "Hello, Amelia Bedelia! How's my favorite daughter?"

"I'm your only daughter," she said.

"Shhhh!" said her father as they sat down together on the steps. He leaned close, and in a fake whisper he said, "Don't

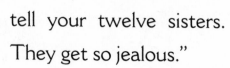

tell your twelve sisters. They get so jealous."

The thought of having twelve sisters was so preposterous that it made Amelia Bedelia smile.

"So, how was school?" asked her father.

"School was fine," said Amelia Bedelia. "Recess was terrible."

"Be glad you still have recess," he said. "I wish I did. I'm glad it's Friday."

"How's work?" asked Amelia Bedelia.

"Another day, another dollar," he said.

"You need a raise, Dad," said Amelia Bedelia.

"I'm just bringing home the bacon," he

said. "Keeping the wolf from our door."

"Save the bacon for tomorrow," said Amelia Bedelia. "We're having chicken tonight."

Her father's stomach growled loudly.

"Yipes," said Amelia Bedelia. "Sounds like you brought home a wolf with the bacon."

"Wolves love bacon," he said, patting his stomach. "I'll huff, and I'll puff, and—"

"I'll blow your house down!" shouted Amelia Bedelia.

BANG!

BANG went their front door as it swung open and hit the side of the house. Amelia Bedelia and her father jumped up.

"Hey, you two!" said Amelia Bedelia's mother from the doorway. "I'm struggling to fix dinner, and here are my best helpers, sitting around having recess."

"I wish," said Amelia Bedelia's father.

"I don't," said Amelia Bedelia.

"Dad, could you carve the chicken for us?" asked Amelia Bedelia's mother. "And Amelia Bedelia, please fill the glasses with water."

"Maybe you should install a water fountain," said Amelia Bedelia.

"Don't be silly," said her

mother. "Who needs a water fountain when I've got you?"

Amelia Bedelia's heart sank, but she did what she was told.

During dinner, Amelia Bedelia told her parents what had happened at recess. She tried to laugh about it, but her parents weren't laughing. They were glancing at each other, the way parents do when they want to talk without kids around.

Amelia Bedelia finished her story by saying, "So I don't feel like filling up water glasses right now, like a water fountain."

"I'm so sorry, sweetie," said her mother. "I didn't mean to hurt your feelings."

"I know," said Amelia Bedelia as she got up from the table. "I'm going to bed. This day has been way too long." She cleared her place and headed to her room.

Chapter 3

Little Pitchers Have Red Ears

Amelia Bedelia tried her best to go to sleep, but it was way too early for that. Plus, she kept hearing her mother and father saying her name, again and again.

Was something wrong?

Was she in trouble?

21

Why were they talking about her?

Amelia Bedelia slipped out of bed and tiptoed down the hall to the top of the stairs. She poked her face between the spindles on the stairway. Now she could

hear everything her parents were saying.

"Amelia Bedelia seems fine to me," said her mother. "But maybe she's having coordination problems."

What kind of problems? Amelia Bedelia looked down at her pajamas. The bottoms matched the top perfectly.

All her outfits were coordinated. She loved matching colors and patterns and—

"She could get stronger," said her father. "You know, get in shape."

Amelia Bedelia looked at herself again. This *was* her shape, the only shape

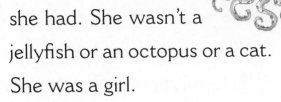

she had. She wasn't a jellyfish or an octopus or a cat. She was a girl.

"Maybe she's just not that interested in sports," said her mother.

Amelia Bedelia almost shouted "Bingo!" She liked sports, but she wasn't crazy about them. Why should she be? In her last try at sports, she had come in second to a crummy water fountain. And now her own parents thought she should get coordinated into a new shape.

"One thing is certain," said her mother. "The corners of her mouth are droopy. That means that our cupcake is unhappy."

"Unhappy!" exclaimed her father.

"*Shhh!*" said her mother. "She'll hear

Shhh!!

you. Little pitchers have big ears."

Amelia Bedelia was puzzled. Had she heard that right? Did her mom want Amelia Bedelia to be a pitcher and play baseball? Or was she saying that Amelia Bedelia had big ears?

"She has lots of friends," said her father in a quieter voice. "All the kids love her."

"True," said her mother. "But if you were always the last one picked for a team, you might not love yourself."

Her parents were talking softly now, so Amelia Bedelia had to strain to hear them. She pressed her face between the spindles as far as she could and tilted her ear toward the kitchen. She caught words like "self-confidence" and "sports camp."

Then she heard a pop. *Pop . . . pop-pop! POP-POP-POP!* Her mom was making popcorn for just the two of them.

The wonderful aroma of freshly popped popcorn wafted upstairs. What torture! Inhaling deeply, Amelia Bedelia pushed her face against the spindles until . . . *POP!* Her entire head went through!

Amelia Bedelia yanked her head back. *YEOW!* Her ears were caught. Her mom was right again. Her ears *were* too big for her own good.

She could hear her parents clearly now, but she couldn't pay attention. She was too busy twisting and turning her head and trying to pull it out from between the spindles. No luck. She heard her name and something about golf.

Then Amelia Bedelia heard her father say, "I've got an early tee time. Let's hit the sack."

Before Amelia Bedelia could wonder why her father was going to a tea party and punching a bag, her parents began turning off lights. *Yipes,* she thought. *They're coming upstairs!*

Her parents would see her head protruding from the stairway like that stuffed deer head decorating the family room in her friend Roger's house.

Amelia Bedelia was so desperate that she did a really gross thing. She spit on her fingers and then rubbed the spit behind her ears to make them slick. Then she steadily pulled her head back until . . . *POP!* Freedom!

As the lights went out in the kitchen, Amelia Bedelia scrambled down the hall and jumped back into bed. She dove under the covers and shut her eyes.

Seconds later her parents tiptoed into her room and stood right next to her bed.

Her dad leaned down to kiss her good-night and his hand brushed her ear. Then he felt her other ear.

"Hey, honey," he whispered, "Amelia Bedelia's ears feel hot."

"Hmmmm," said her mother as she pushed the hair off Amelia Bedelia's

forehead, then gently touched her ears. "No fever, but we were talking about her, so now her ears are burning."

Amelia Bedelia didn't say a word. After her parents left quietly, she and her fiery ears kept pretending to be asleep until at last she was.

Chapter 4

Hole in None

Amelia Bedelia hoped she was having a nightmare. If this were a nightmare, she knew she could open her eyes and it would be over. But no, it was much worse. This was reality. Her father was waking her up way too early on a Saturday morning.

"Rise and shine,

sleepyhead!" said Amelia Bedelia's father. "We've got a date with a golf course!"

Amelia Bedelia rubbed her eyes. Both her parents were in her room.

"We're going to play golf," said her father. "Actually, you'll get to watch me play golf, you lucky girl."

"I'd rather watch paint drying," said Amelia Bedelia.

"Don't be cranky, sweetie," said her mother. "You'll get outside, walk around, get some exercise. . . ."

"Hurry and get dressed," said her dad. "Tee time is eight o'clock."

On the way to the golf course, Amelia Bedelia's father told her all about the history of golf. The game began in Scotland, so Amelia Bedelia figured that was why they'd have tea first.

They parked their car at the course and picked out a snazzy golf cart.

"Climb in," said her father.

"Dad," said Amelia Bedelia. "Aren't we supposed to walk . . . you know, exercise?"

33

Her father looked around, then whispered, "Don't tell Mom and I'll let you drive."

"Deal," said Amelia Bedelia, jumping in beside him.

They drove to a small hill, stopped the cart, and got out.

"I'm thirsty," said Amelia Bedelia. "Is it tea time yet?"

"There's a bag of tees right there," said her father. "Help yourself, and hand me one."

Amelia picked up the bag. She didn't see any tea, just pointy little pieces of colored wood. She handed a red one to her dad. He stuck it in the ground and balanced his golf ball on top of it.

"Golf lesson number one," said her father. "You have to address the ball."

"Address the ball?" said Amelia Bedelia. "Are we mailing it somewhere?"

"No, silly," said her father. "Just stand like this, then you can address it properly. . . ."

Amelia Bedelia stood just like her dad. Then she bent down to

the ball. Using her most polite, grown-up voice, she said, "Hello, Mister Ball. Are you ready to play a little golf today?"

Next, Amelia Bedelia's father demonstrated how to swing the club he called his driver. Amelia Bedelia thought this was weird. Wasn't *she* his driver? Then he hit the ball for real— *WHACK*—

and sent it flying into the air, far, far away.

"Wow!" said Amelia Bedelia. "What were you aiming for?"

"The green," said her father.

Amelia Bedelia turned in a complete circle. "But everything around us is green," she said. "The grass, bushes, trees . . ."

"See that tiny patch of grass?" her father asked, pointing into the distance.

"With the little flag on a stick?"
asked Amelia Bedelia.

"Yup," he said. "That's the first hole.
Now it's your turn to drive."

They hopped back into the cart.
"Hang on, Dad!" said Amelia Bedelia as
they sped away.

She drove them to the ball he had just hit. Driving was fun, but they were still a long way from that flag.

"Please hand me a wood," said Amelia Bedelia's father.

Amelia Bedelia looked around for a stick or a branch.

"On second thought," he said, "hand me an iron."

"You don't need one," she said. "Your clothes look fine. They're not wrinkly."

"This is an iron in golf," her father said, reaching for a club with a metal head. He used it to hit the ball again and again. And again. Each time they got closer to the green and the flag.

Amelia Bedelia followed her father in the cart, occasionally doing big loop de loops.

At last he announced, "I'm going to chip the ball now."

Amelia Bedelia was certain that a chipped ball didn't roll as well as a perfectly round ball. They'd done an experiment about this in science. He

LOW

must not have chipped the ball much, because it landed on the green and rolled smoothly toward the little hole with the flag poking out of it.

Her dad got out his putter and walked up to the ball. "When I hit the ball," he said, "pull out the pin."

"What pin?" said Amelia Bedelia. "A safety pin? A rolling pin?"

"No," said her father. "In golf, the pin is the flag. Pull the flag out of the hole."

He tapped the ball. It began rolling downhill, picking up speed and curving perfectly toward the flag. Amelia Bedelia pulled out the flag and put her foot in front of the hole. The ball bounced off her shoe.

"What did you do that for?" yelled her father.

"To keep the ball from falling into the hole," said Amelia Bedelia. "You're welcome!"

"That's the point of golf," he said. "That hole is the cup!"

"If that's the cup," said Amelia Bedelia, "you can forget about teatime. I'm not thirsty anymore."

Amelia Bedelia was glad her father only played nine holes. The last one was a water hole, where the ball had to be hit over a pond. And there were no refreshments, unless you counted the

slimy green pond, which she did not.

Her father was about to hit the ball when Amelia Bedelia noticed something. "Hey, Dad," she said, "that ball you're using looks disgusting!"

Her dad explained that he often hit the ball into the pond and lost it there.

"I've lost more balls than I can count in that pond," her father said. "That's why I'm using this yucky old one. I won't miss it if I lose it."

He was swinging his club when

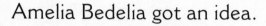

Amelia Bedelia got an idea.

"Wait!" she hollered.

She was too late. The ball sailed away.

"Amelia Bedelia," her father said sternly. "Never interrupt an athlete who is hitting or throwing or catching a ball. It's an important rule of good sportsmanship. I didn't even see where my ball went."

He teed up another one and hit it onto the green. Amelia Bedelia wanted to go wading into the pond after his ball, but now it didn't matter. On his second putt, the ball fell into the cup. When Amelia Bedelia reached in to pull it out, she made a discovery.

"Hey," she said. "There was already a ball in here!"

She held it up for him to see, and they both recognized it. It was the beat-up ball

he had hit first. Amelia Bedelia's father looked stunned. Then he waved his putter around and threw his hat in the air. She had never seen him so mad. Then she realized he was happy. Really, really happy.

"Yippee—a hole in one!" he yelled,
dancing around the cup. "I got a hole in
one!"

What a wild tea party! thought Amelia
Bedelia.

Chapter 5

Downward-Facing Finally

On Sunday afternoon, Amelia Bedelia found her mother practicing yoga in the guest bedroom. She looked so calm and so serene. It was relaxing just watching her. A few minutes later, Finally came in and lay down next to Amelia Bedelia's mother on the floor.

"What do you like about yoga?" asked Amelia Bedelia.

"It keeps me in shape," said her mother.

"How do you change shape?" Amelia Bedelia asked. "What shape are you now?"

Her mother was down on her hands and knees with her back straight. "This is called table pose," she said.

"I get it," said Amelia Bedelia. "Your back is the top of the table, and your legs are the legs of the table."

"My arms are legs too," said her mother, arching her back up into the air. "Now what do I look like?"

Amelia Bedelia shrugged.

"Like a croquet hoop."

"This is cat pose," said her mother.

"Shhhh!" said Amelia Bedelia. "Don't say that word in front of Finally!"

"Here's one for her," said Amelia

Bedelia's mother as she straightened her legs and put her bottom up in the air until she looked like an upside-down letter V. "This pose is called downward-facing dog. Try it."

Amelia Bedelia got down on the floor and tried the pose. Finally stood up and

stretched the same way, poking her furry rear end high in the air.

Amelia Bedelia and her mother looked at Finally, then at each other.

"Finally does a better downward-facing dog pose than either of us," said her mother.

"Woof!" agreed Amelia Bedelia.

They began giggling and couldn't stop. Finally started to bark. She ran under their bellies, like a ball zipping through a pair of croquet hoops, until Amelia Bedelia and her mom collapsed on the floor together.

As her mother rolled up her yoga mat,

she said, "Thank you for going with your dad to play golf, sweetie. It meant a lot to him that you saw him get that hole in one."

"It was fun," said Amelia Bedelia. "I learned new words."

Her mother stopped smiling. "New words?" she asked. "What new words?"

Amelia Bedelia could tell that her mom was trying to keep a calm yoga voice.

"Golf words," said Amelia Bedelia. "Like the word 'hook.' It's not like a fishhook. It's when you hit the ball and it curves back to the left and gets lost in the bushes. Then he had a slice."

"Pizza?" asked her mother.

"Nope," said Amelia Bedelia. "This

slice is when you hit the ball and it veers to the right and bounces off a tree."

"I see," said her mother. "What happens when your dad hits the ball and it goes straight down the middle?"

Amelia Bedelia smiled and said, "He hollers 'Hooray!' and jumps in the air."

Her mother laughed.

"Hey," said Amelia Bedelia. "Where is Dad?"

"It's Sunday afternoon, cupcake," said Amelia Bedelia's mother with an exaggerated shrug. "I wonder where on earth your father could be. . . ."

Amelia Bedelia understood immediately.

Chapter 6

Get the  Cents Back

Amelia Bedelia went downstairs to the family room. Her father was snug as a bug in his recliner. He was eating chips and dip and watching football.

Amelia Bedelia sat on the footstool. She did her best to look interested in the game, which was just beginning. Football had always baffled her, but her dad loved it, so she was open to giving it another try.

"Why is that guy dressed like a zebra?" she asked, pointing at the man in a black-and-white-striped shirt.

"That's the ref—the referee," said her father. "He makes sure the players follow the rules. See, he just flipped a quarter to decide which team will kick the ball to the other team."

"Who are those two other guys on the field with him, the ones wearing numbers?" asked Amelia Bedelia.

"They're quarterbacks," said her dad.

"Did Zebra Guy give them back their quarters?" asked Amelia Bedelia.

"No," said her father. "Each team tries to get the other team's quarterback."

Amelia Bedelia was amazed. "Do you mean those guys knock into one another just trying to get a quarter back?"

Her dad laughed. "Those guys get paid millions of dollars to tackle one another," he said.

"That's a lot of quarters," said Amelia Bedelia, dipping a chip into the dip. Once the game began,

4 3

Amelia Bedelia's father acted as though he was playing too.

He yelled at the TV, telling the players where to run, when to pass, and how to tackle. He spent every minute cheering and booing and even jumping in the air and grabbing his hair.

"Maybe you ought to play football instead of golf, Dad," said Amelia Bedelia.

Her father was not listening. "Uh-oh," he said. "Our quarterback is behind the eight ball."

Gosh, thought Amelia Bedelia, *even the ball has a number.* No wonder she was clueless when it came to football! It was all about math. There were scores and

$\div 4 = ?$

penalties and measurements involved. Football players were covered in numbers, and some players were even fractions. She could hear Mrs. Robbins now: "If a quarterback has the number twelve on his uniform, and you divide that by four, what number is he really? If a halfback

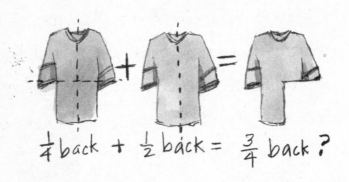

$\frac{1}{4}$ back + $\frac{1}{2}$ back = $\frac{3}{4}$ back?

has the number twenty on his uniform, is he really a ten or a five?"

Amelia Bedelia discovered that the game itself was divided into quarters.

At halftime she and her dad watched a band marching around the field in fancy geometric formations. Worse still, the announcers kept talking about numbers called statistics, measuring how these teams were doing compared to other teams and past games. Numbers kept pouring off the screen, flowing out of the speakers, flooding the family room with a tidal wave of math that left her floating on her footstool in a sea of arithmetic. Thank

goodness for the yummy chips and dip!

Then Amelia Bedelia heard a sound that was music to her ears.

"Z-z-z-z-z-z-z-z . . ."

Her dad had fallen asleep. She gently slid the remote out of his hand. She lowered the volume so she wouldn't wake him up while she was changing the channel to something good.

Amelia Bedelia found a nature show about a troop of gorillas. They were fighting over a coconut. A silverback took it away from the others and ran off with it. Some zebras were grazing in background. It looked like a football game, without any numbers.

Just then, her dad snorted and opened his eyes groggily. His glasses fell off.

"What's the score?" he asked, squinting at the screen.

"Twenty-one to fourteen," said Amelia Bedelia, remembering the score of the football game before she switched the channel.

"Who's ahead?' he asked.

"The team with twenty-one points," she said.

"That's right," said her dad, rolling over to resume his nap. "That's how football works. *Z-z-z-z-z-z.*"

Amelia Bedelia couldn't blame him. This weekend had worn her out too. She couldn't wait to get back to school and away from sports for a while.

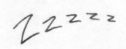

Chapter 7

Marathon, Pentathlon, and On and On . . .

On Monday, Amelia Bedelia discovered one good thing about spending her Saturday on a golf course. None of the other kids in her class had ever played golf—miniature golf, maybe, but not real grown-up golf. Amelia Bedelia told everyone how she'd helped her father get a hole in one.

"Whoa," said Skip. "My dad would give anything for that."

Even Dawn was impressed. "*I'd* give anything for that!" she said.

With sports out of the way, Amelia Bedelia was ready for social studies. She loved anything to do with history, because it had already happened. There were no surprises. She loved ancient history most of all, because that stuff had happened so long ago, it was . . . well . . . ancient!

"I've got a surprise for you!" announced Mr. Tobin, their social studies teacher. "Today we start our study of ancient

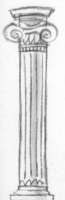

Greece. We will reach back thousands of years, travel across time and space to bring those times into the present. We will learn about Greek inventions and food and families and the Greek gods and myths. We will relive those ancient times by holding our own Greek Games, an athletic competition featuring a variety of sports from ancient Greece."

While the entire class erupted in cheers and shouts, Amelia Bedelia sat in stunned silence. She was doomed. There was no escaping sports. Sports had been around for thousands of years. Fortunately, she wasn't the only one worrying.

"What sports did

65

the ancient Greeks play?" asked Teddy.

"Well," said Mr. Tobin, "the first marathon was run by a Greek messenger."

"Are we running a marathon?" asked Holly.

"Certainly not," said Mr. Tobin. "A marathon is more than twenty-six miles."

"Wow," said Cliff. "That messenger must have gotten a medal."

"Actually," said Mr. Tobin, "right after he delivered the message, he died."

"Died?" said Clay. "Actually died?"

"Don't worry," said Mr. Tobin. "We're going to do an ancient pentathlon, just like they did back in 708 BC."

"I hope it's a shorter race," said Clay.

"It is," said Mr. Tobin. "Remember

your geometry—also invented
by the Greeks. A *penta*gon has

Pentagon

five sides. So a *penta*thlon has
five events, one of which
is a short race. You'll only have to run
a hundred meters. That's about one
hundred and nine yards."

Everyone except Amelia Bedelia
breathed a sigh of relief. Some of the yards

Mrs. Adams's yard

Our yard

$+102$ more!! $= 109$ yards!

in her neighborhood were really big. She couldn't imagine what it would be like to run through one hundred and nine of them. She'd have to stop and rest, for sure.

"What are the other four events?" asked Angel.

Mr. Tobin turned to the blackboard and made a list. "A pentathlon includes the hundred-meter run, long jump, wrestling, discus throw, and last but not least, javelin," he said.

discus

"Javelin?" asked Clay. "We get to throw a spear?"

javelin

"You bet," said Mr. Tobin. "But we will do it safely, I assure you."

Mr. Tobin spent the rest of social studies answering questions and talking about how important sports were in ancient Greece. He showed them pictures with statues of athletes throwing a discus and a javelin. He also showed them pictures of big vases decorated with images of

discus

long jump

wrestling

footrace

javelin

athletes wrestling or jumping.

Clay raised his hand. "Mr. Tobin," he said, "those ancient athletes are naked. Can we wear clothes at our pentathlon?"

Mr. Tobin waited for the laughter to die down before he answered. "Yes, on one condition," he said. "Your assignment is to wear chitons and sandals, just like the Greek boys and girls would have done. Look, here's a picture."

Chip said, "It's a toga party!" Everyone cheered.

"Save that for the pentathlon," said Mr. Tobin. Then he showed them one last picture. It was an image of a big plate that was in a museum. Greek athletes were

← chiton

← sandals

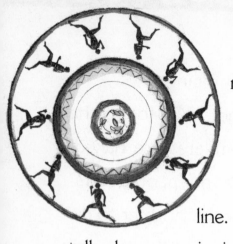

running in a footrace around the rim of the plate. There was no starting point or finish line. It was impossible to tell who was winning and who was losing or who was ahead and who was behind. They had been chasing one another around the rim of that plate, in an endless circle, for thousands of years, just for the pure joy of running. Amelia Bedelia loved it.

If the ancient Greeks were choosing teams, would they have chosen her? Water fountains hadn't been invented yet. Would the team captain have picked an animal skin filled with cool water before choosing Amelia Bedelia?

Chapter 8

On Your Mark, Get Set . . . STOP!

The first practice session for the pentathlon took place on an unusually hot and humid day. Amelia Bedelia and her classmates were sent out to the lower field for gym.

TWEEEEEEET!

Some kids jumped, and others covered their ears. Everyone spun around. A

young woman was standing before them, a clipboard in one hand and a water bottle in the other. She had a large silver whistle between her lips. She let the whistle fall and dangle from a lanyard around her neck.

"Afternoon, kids. My name is Mrs. Thompson. You may call me Mrs. Thompson or Coach Thompson, but I prefer just Coach. I usually work with the older kids, but Mr. Tobin has asked me to get you in shape for your Greek Games. Any questions?"

Rose raised her hand. "It's pretty hot. Can we sit in the shade until—"

"Nope," said Coach Thompson. "Now line up, and let's have a look at you."

Everyone shuffled into a wavy, lumpy line. They resembled an anaconda that had stuffed itself at Thanksgiving.

Coach Thompson clapped sharply

three times. "Come on, come on! Move it! Line up alphabetically," she called out.

That was easy for Amelia Bedelia. Her name put her at the head of the line. She would be the first to be inspected by Mrs. Thompson.

"Hello," said Mrs. Thompson.

"Hello, Just Coach," said Amelia Bedelia.

"What did you call me?" asked Mrs. Thompson.

"Just Coach," said Amelia Bedelia. "You said that's what you prefer."

"Not just," said Mrs. Thompson. "Only Coach."

"Okay, Only Coach," said Amelia Bedelia.

"*Coach*," said Mrs. Thompson. "No

'only' or 'just' before it.
I'm Coach, period."

Amelia Bedelia thought about asking Coach Period why she kept changing her name, but she decided to nod instead.

Coach Period asked for her name and wrote it down on her clipboard. "Amelia Bedelia," she said.

"That's right," said Amelia Bedelia.

"That's alphabetical," said Coach Period, continuing down the line.

"Now," she said, when she had recorded everyone's name. "Running is fundamental to fitness. I want to see how fast you kids are. You're all going to run to that water fountain and back while I time you."

A shiver ran through Amelia Bedelia.

Not the water fountain again! This was a bad omen.

"Okay," said Coach Period. "The race will begin when I say, 'On your mark, get set, go!'"

Amelia Bedelia took off.

"Amelia Bedelia! Stop!" yelled the coach. *TWEEEEEET!* "Come back!"

Amelia Bedelia turned around and

TWEET!

TWeeeeeet!   tweet

trotted back. She could hear snickering. She crouched down again, breathing hard.

"Haven't you ever raced before?" said Coach Period. "Wait until I say the word 'Go.'"

Amelia Bedelia took off again, sprinting even faster.

TWEEEET!!!

TWEEEEEET!

"Get back here, Amelia Bedelia!" hollered Coach.

Amelia Bedelia stopped and walked back to her place in line, even more out of breath. Now everyone was giggling.

Coach Period looked right at Amelia Bedelia and said, "Do not move a muscle until I say you-know-what word.

"On your mark . . . get set—"

"Coach," interrupted Cliff. "This is an emergency. I *really* need to go to the bathroom."

Coach Period turned to Cliff and hollered, "Okay, already. Go!"

Amelia Bedelia took off as fast as she could. The coach stood there dumb-struck. Then she started her stopwatch and said, "Well, what's everyone waiting for? Didn't you hear me say GO?"

The rest of the class took off together like a thundering herd. Holly came in first, as she always did. She was fast. Even with her head start, Amelia Bedelia stumbled

across the finish line in last place, as she always did.

Coach studied her stopwatch. "Let me tell you where you stand," she said, shaking her head.

Amelia Bedelia looked around. No one was standing. Everyone was walking around puffing and panting or lying on the ground gasping and wheezing.

"You all need a lot of conditioning," said Coach, shaking her head.

Amelia Bedelia thought everyone's hair looked great. No one needed more conditioning, especially not Angel. Amelia Bedelia wished she had hair like Angel's.

Amelia Bedelia whispered to Clay, "Do you need hair conditioning?"

"No, thanks," said Clay. "But I could use some air-conditioning."

TWEEEET!

"Follow me, young Greeks!" yelled Coach.

TWeeeeeet!

Then she led them in a jog around the field—*five times* around the field!

"It's like a pentajog," said Amelia Bedelia to Rose.

"It's a nightmare," said Rose.

Coach ran ahead, but *backward*, giving them advice and encouragement until it was time to return to the classroom.

Chapter 9

The Hundred-Meter Dash

Mr. Tobin was drawing a picture of two winding snakes on the board when the class staggered back into the room.

"Whoa, you all look exhausted," he said. "I asked Coach not to make you guys run a marathon on your very first day of training."

"She ran us into the ground," said Joy.

"My blisters have blisters," said Heather, taking off her shoes to rub her feet.

"Phew!" said Clay. "Did a skunk pass by?"

Heather glared at him and put her shoes back on.

"Did you hear what Coach told us?" asked Skip. "She said, 'Sometimes you have to go the extra mile.' I've never run even one mile before today, and she expects me to run an extra one!"

"Tell that to that dead messenger," said Cliff. "If he had stopped at twenty-five miles instead of going for twenty-six, he might still be alive today."

Cliff and Skip laughed.

"That's so dumb," said Penny. "He lived and died thousands of years ago. You make it sound like you could see him jogging in the park right this minute."

"Yeah, don't listen to Cliff," said Wade. "He totally missed the first race. When the going got tough, Cliff was going to the bathroom!"

"Oh, yeah?" said Cliff. He tackled Wade, and they rolled on the ground.

"Break it up, guys," said Mr. Tobin. "Save that for the wrestling ring at the Greek Games, shall we? Before we learn what it was like to live in ancient Greece, I'll make a deal with you. I'm willing to forget about assigning homework for a few days if you'll use the extra time to do sports homework—go jogging, play games, and get more exercise."

"You're giving us a vacation from homework?" said Clay.

"Let's call it a homework hiatus," said Mr. Tobin.

"My uncle had an operation to repair his hiatus," said Pat. "He's fine now."

Amelia Bedelia knew that Pat couldn't be right because of the way Penny was rolling her eyes. Penny was going to be a doctor, so she knew more than anyone in class about the human body. Also, it was clear that Mr. Tobin was trying really hard not to laugh.

"Thank you for sharing some family history, Pat," said Mr. Tobin, smiling.

"Let's talk about medicine and the ancient Greeks. The Greeks were some of the first doctors the world had known. Hippocrates is considered the father of medicine, founding the first medical school around 400 BC. And we get our symbol for medicine from a Greek god."

Amelia Bedelia saw Penny perk up and start taking notes. Like Penny, she was really interested in what Mr. Tobin was saying. But her eyes kept straying to the list that was still on the board, the five events of the pentathlon. She had never thrown a discus, and her parents probably weren't going to let her toss a javelin around

TODAY IS
400 B

FIRST DOCTOR'S
APPOINTMENT

their backyard. But she could certainly practice the hundred-meter dash. In fact, she knew exactly where she could find at least a hundred meters in a row.

After school, Amelia Bedelia dropped her backpack at home, ate  a quick snack with Finally, and explained her sports homework to her mom. Then she jogged downtown.

Main Street was several blocks long, with parking meters on both sides. She counted thirty-one on one side of the street and twenty-nine on the other side. The numbers weren't equal because there were two driveways on the twenty-nine

side, where people couldn't park. She found the other forty meters she needed on two side streets.

Now came the tricky part. She had to time herself so she would arrive at the crosswalk just as the light changed. That way the cars would be stopped and the WALK sign lit up, and she would be able to cross safely. Phew! Running was complicated. Did the ancient

Greeks have to deal with this?

On her first try, she got past the thirty-one meters but had to wait at the light. On her next attempt, the crosswalk sign was flashing DON'T WALK. She ran in place until she realized that she was not walking—she was *running*. So she sprinted across the street before the light changed.

Amelia Bedelia was counting off the next set of meters—thirty-two, thirty-three, thirty-four, thirty-five—when she heard a sound that brought her to a screeching halt.

TWEEEEET!

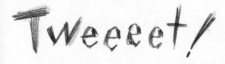

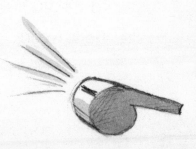

Oh, no! Coach Period must have tracked her down! Turning around took every bit of courage Amelia Bedelia could muster. Uh-oh! It wasn't Coach Period. It was way worse. It was Officer O'Brien!

Amelia Bedelia really hoped the policeman didn't remember her. She'd had a run-in with him in the park after picking a flower bed clean and then selling the bouquet for twenty dollars. But that was another story.

"What's going on?" said Officer O'Brien. "Did someone tell you to go play in traffic?"

"No, sir," said Amelia Bedelia. "I'm running a hundred meters for homework."

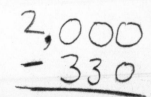

Officer O'Brien looked down the row of meters, smiled, and said, "There's a big difference between a hundred meters and a hundred parking meters." He paced off the distance between two parking meters. "That's about twenty feet." He wrote TWENTY FEET on the sidewalk with the chalk he used to mark the tires of parked cars.

"If you multiply twenty feet by one hundred parking meters, you get 2,000 feet. But one hundred meters (the distance) is only about 330 feet. So when you run past a hundred parking meters, how much extra have you run?"

Officer O'Brien handed his chalk to Amelia Bedelia. She wondered if he was

$$2{,}000 - 330$$

friends with Mrs. Robbins. They could do math together. She wrote 330 under the 2,000 and subtracted it.

"Hey," said Amelia Bedelia. "I ran 1,670 feet too far."

The policeman nodded. "If I were you," he said, "I'd set up a course 330 feet long in your neighborhood. And Amelia

Bedelia," he added, "when 'Don't Walk' is flashing, that doesn't mean dash across the street before the light changes. 'Don't Walk' means stop."

"Thanks, Officer O'Brien," she said.

Then Officer O'Brien picked a flower from a nearby planter. "Take this to your mother," he said, smiling.

Amelia Bedelia was relieved that her only problem with Officer O'Brien had been a math problem.

Chapter 10

Throw like a Girl, Shake like a Boy

Amelia Bedelia set up a running course as soon as she got home. Finally raced along beside her, and she wished she could run as fast as her dog. That's the only chance she'd have of beating anyone, especially Holly, who was faster than every girl *and* boy in the class.

Amelia Bedelia practiced her

hundred-meter dash every day that week. But how, she wondered, would she ever learn to wrestle? At a time like this, an older brother or sister would come in handy. Even a younger brother or sister would help.

She'd asked her parents for a baby brother or sister. She'd gotten her own dog instead. So she decided that Finally was going to be her wrestling partner. After all, Amelia Bedelia's favorite parts of nature shows were the wrestling matches between the young animals. She loved to watch lion cubs shoving each other around or a pair of bear

cubs squabbling over honey. They were so cute!

Finally was taking a nap. Amelia Bedelia got down on her knees and snuck up behind her. She grabbed Finally's favorite chew toy, a blue plastic duck. Finally opened one eye.

"Come get it!" Amelia Bedelia teased.

Finally latched on to the duck and away they went, tugging back and forth, up and down, from side to side, then rolling around on the ground together. Finally loved helping Amelia Bedelia with her homework.

Finally did teach Amelia Bedelia one move. They were both tugging at the toy, straining with all their might, when Finally suddenly let go. Amelia Bedelia went tumbling backward. She dropped the duck in surprise. Finally scooped it up,

her tail wagging in triumph.

"Smart girl!" said Amelia Bedelia. "Want to go for a walk?"

It was a gorgeous day, so the park was packed with people and dogs enjoying the weather. "Hi, Amelia Bedelia!" said Diana. She was walking a bunch of dogs with her boyfriend, Eric.

"We just saw Charlie walking Pierre."

Amelia Bedelia had once helped Diana with her dog-walking service, and Eric had helped Amelia Bedelia and her friend Charlie solve a poodle problem. Maybe Eric could help her again.

"Hey, Eric," said Amelia Bedelia. "Do you know how to throw a javelin?"

Eric laughed, but Diana laughed louder. "Well," said Eric, "I was in the military a while ago, but not *that* long ago. Why do you want to throw a javelin?"

Amelia Bedelia told them all about the upcoming pentathlon and how Finally was helping her learn to wrestle.

"I once took a self-defense course," said Diana. "I'll show you what I know."

Eric held the leashes while Diana and Amelia Bedelia headed to a grassy spot.

"If you have to wrestle someone bigger or stronger," said Diana, "you can use their size and strength against them."

She showed Amelia Bedelia how to push against opponents and then pull them off balance. It was the same move that Finally had taught her.

"Remember," said Diana as she and Eric headed off to deliver the dogs to their owners. "Always stand tall!"

"Thanks for helping me!" yelled Amelia Bedelia.

Just then Amelia Bedelia spotted Charlie. Actually, Pierre saw Finally first and came running to greet them with a tennis ball in his mouth. Pierre dropped the ball at Amelia Bedelia's feet.

"Hi, Charlie," said Amelia Bedelia.

"Hey, Amelia Bedelia!" said Charlie. "Looks like Pierre wants you to throw the ball for him."

Amelia Bedelia picked up the ball and threw it with all her might. It soared through the air for about ten feet before it landed on the ground,

bounced once, and rolled a couple of feet more.

Pierre looked at the ball, then back at Amelia Bedelia. He had a funny look on his furry face that said, That's the best you can do? Even Finally looked embarrassed.

"Hah," Charlie blurted out. "You throw like a girl!"

Amelia Bedelia's face turned bright red. She felt angry and ashamed and confused and uncomfortable all at once.

"That's right, Charlie," said Amelia

Bedelia. "I throw like a girl, because I *am* a girl. And so is Finally. Which is just fine. But since you have a problem with that, we're leaving!"

Charlie caught up with her and grabbed her arm. She was tempted to use one of

her new wrestling moves on him, but he was already apologizing.

"Amelia Bedelia," he said, "I'm sorry.

I'm just surprised you don't know the secret of throwing."

"What secret?" asked Amelia Bedelia, blinking away her tears.

Charlie showed her how gripping the ball with two fingers gives it a spin that keeps it on track to where it's aimed. "Use your whole body," he said, "not just your arm. Plus, take a few steps so you get the energy from your legs too."

Charlie helped her with each move until she had it down. "Now here's the secret," he said, almost in a whisper. "Cross your right leg over your left on the last step. When you untwist, all the power of your body goes into the throw, like this."

Charlie gripped the ball, jogged a few steps, twisted his right leg over his left,

and rocketed the ball into the air.

Pierre and Finally looked at each other, then went racing off to retrieve it.

"Wow!" said Amelia Bedelia. "That's great!"

When the dogs came

back with the ball, Amelia
Bedelia wiped the puppy
spit off it and tried Charlie's
secret method. It worked!
She'd never thrown that far before.
"Wow!" she hollered, jumping into the
air.

"We're friends again, right?" asked
Charlie, holding out his hand.

"I'll always be your friend," said Amelia
Bedelia. "Even though you shake hands
like a boy."

They laughed, parting ways, their
dogs leading them home. Amelia Bedelia's
mother was waiting on the front steps,
holding what used to be her best cake pans.

Eeew! Dog slobber!!

Chapter 11

Greece-y Pan Quakes

Amelia Bedelia's mother was holding a pan in each hand, waving them around like those workers at the airport who direct planes to their parking spots.

"Young lady," said her mother. "What did you do to my cake pans?"

"It was for homework," said Amelia Bedelia. "Rose and Daisy and I needed something shaped like a discus so we could practice our throwing."

"You threw my baking pans around the yard?" asked Amelia Bedelia's mother.

"Mom, they're made of metal," said Amelia Bedelia. "They didn't break."

"They're dented," said her mother. "Here comes your father. Let's see what he has to say."

Amelia Bedelia's father had heard

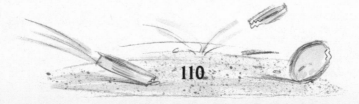

them arguing a block away. He walked up to his house with all the enthusiasm of someone headed over a cliff.

"What are you two up to?" he asked.

"I'm up to four feet and one inch," said Amelia Bedelia. "Mom is probably the same height she was when you left this morning."

"But I've had it up to here with these

Greek Games," said her mother, indicating a level just above her head. "Look at my cake pans."

"Amelia Bedelia will have to pay for new pans," said her father.

"I need them tonight," said Amelia Bedelia's mother. "I'm baking cakes for the class picnic after the pentathlon."

"Besides dented discus cakes," he asked, "what else is on the menu? I hope the food isn't Greece-y."

Amelia Bedelia and her mother groaned.

"Daaad," said Amelia Bedelia.

"Then you should love what we're having tonight," said Amelia Bedelia's mother. "We're eating vegetarian."

Amelia Bedelia's father made a

face. "I've never gotten used to eating vegetarians," he said. "Those folks taste like broccoli that's gone bad."

"Daaad . . ." A shiver ran down Amelia Bedelia's spine. "Don't say that," she said. "I will totally lose my appetite."

"Sorry, cupcake. Let's feast on rabbit food," he said, clapping his hands and rubbing them together with fake excitement.

"Honey, I did make you a couch potato," said Amelia Bedelia's mother.

That was his favorite—a double-stuffed baked potato with two kinds of cheese.

"Gangway!" he said, running up the steps.

Zzzz

Chapter 12

High Pentas All Around

The next day was the day of the Greek Games. Mr. Tobin, Coach, and everyone in Amelia Bedelia's class arrived at school dressed in chitons or tunics and sandals. Amelia Bedelia and some of her friends even fixed their hair in ancient hairstyles. For fun, they posed like the Greeks pictured on ancient vases and pottery.

When it was time for the pentathlon to begin, they traded in their sandals for sneakers. The class paraded outside, carrying flags and banners representing the five events of the pentathlon. They marched down to the lower field, where parents and some of the younger kids at their school had already gathered, cheering, to watch the games.

The first event was the discus.

"You'll get two chances to throw the discus," said Coach. "I'll record every throw, and we will officially mark on the field the two longest throws made."

Amelia Bedelia was tenth in line. Her first throw was okay. It wasn't the longest throw, and it wasn't the shortest. It was right in the middle. Then she spotted her mother in the crowd. Amelia Bedelia wanted to show her mom that she had wrecked her cake pans for an important

reason. She whirled around once, twice, three times. She kept whirling around and around like a tornado.

"Let go, already!" shouted Coach.

Amelia Bedelia did, and the discus went flying up, up, up in a high arc. Then

it came down and struck the ground. It was the longest throw so far. But instead of being happy, Amelia Bedelia was so dizzy that she staggered three steps and fell over, the sky spinning above her. Her mother ran over to make sure she was all right.

"Great throw, sweetheart," whispered her mom as she helped Amelia Bedelia to her feet. "I'm glad my cake pans paid off."

Amelia Bedelia's toss was the longest until Pat threw the discus. Both of his throws were longer than Amelia Bedelia's, so Pat got first place and Amelia Bedelia came in second.

"The most important part of playing

sports is being a good sport," said Mr. Tobin. "That's why we are now going to perform that traditional sporting salute of ancient Greece, the high penta."

Mr. Tobin turned to Pat and gave him a high five. The rest of the class followed suit.

"Nice win, Pat!" said Coach, smiling.

Amelia Bedelia was tired already, and she was not ready for the hundred-meter dash, which was the next event. She was thinking about "pulling a Cliff" and heading to the restroom. She could really use a rest! But her classmates were assembling on the starting line, so she did too. There was the finish line, marked with white tape, just a hundred meters away. She could do it! They all crouched down, ready for the signal.

"On your marks . . . get set . . . GO!"

Holly took the lead right away, with Wade, Teddy, and Dawn hot on her heels, followed by Amelia Bedelia. Then it happened. Wade tripped and fell, causing Teddy and Dawn to tumble down too. Amelia Bedelia jumped over the tangled bunch and kept running. Then Suzanne fell on the pile and a bunch of other kids stumbled too. Holly looked back over her shoulder to see

what the commotion was, and that cost her dearly.

Amelia Bedelia was coming up fast, huffing and puffing. "Slow down, Holly! Slow down, Holly!"

"No way," said Holly as Amelia Bedelia drew alongside her. They were both heading for the finish line, neck and neck. Holly suddenly leaned as far forward as she could, almost falling on her face—but breaking the tape at the finish line before Amelia Bedelia.

"Holly wins by a nose!" shouted Mr. Tobin, who was right there watching.

The crowd went wild!

Amelia Bedelia stretched out her leg muscles as the rest of the class staggered

and limped across the line. She didn't feel
that bad. It wasn't that she wasn't fast
enough. Her real problem
was that her nose was too
short.

On her way to the water
fountain for a drink, Amelia
Bedelia gave Holly a high

penta with each hand. "Congratulations," she said.

"Our first high deca!" said Mr. Tobin. "What an honor!"

The next event, the javelin throw, let everyone catch their breath. Coach and Mr. Tobin cleared the field. Some parents, including Amelia Bedelia's father, stood guard, making sure that no one got hurt. "We don't want any student shish kebobs," he said.

As with the discus toss, each student got two throws. Using Charlie's right-leg-across-left secret throwing technique, Amelia Bedelia threw the javelin farther than any girl and almost any boy. Only Clay hurled it farther down the field. There were high pentas for him, and another second place for Amelia Bedelia.

Chapter 13

A Lonnnnngg Jump to a Short End

Amelia Bedelia hadn't practiced her long jump, except in gym class. As it turned out, she didn't need to. She went running toward the white board where you take off, building up speed before she leaped into the air. As she took off, she heard Coach cry out, "Scratch!"

Amelia Bedelia touched down in the

landing pit. Her arms were windmilling to help her keep her balance, but she couldn't stay upright, and she fell back into the soft sand.

"Sorry," said Mr. Tobin as he measured her jump. "Because you fell backward, I have to measure from where your body hit the sand, not your feet."

Amelia Bedelia jogged back to the

starting block for her next try. When she got there, Coach gave her more bad news.

"You scratched," said Coach.

"Scratched what?" asked Amelia Bedelia. She didn't remember having an itch. Oh, maybe she had scratched some equipment when she took off!

"Your toe slipped over the line before you jumped," said Coach. "I had to disqualify your first attempt. In sports, that's called a 'scratch.' You've got one more try."

Now Amelia Bedelia was nervous. She wasn't worried about winning. She was having too much fun coming in second time after time. She had a runner-up reputation to uphold!

Amelia Bedelia started to run, picking

scratch!

up speed, going faster and faster, but making sure that she didn't go over the line again. She was just about to take off when . . . *TWEEEEEEET!*

"EEEHHH—*YAHHHHHHH!*" screamed Amelia Bedelia.

A blowing whistle always made her jump. She flew into the air, her arms and legs spinning around and around, her feet still running. She soared up and up, flying straight toward Mr. Tobin. She landed far into the pit. Like before, her whole body

began teeter-tottering, knees going in and out, arms swinging back and forth. She struggled against gravity to keep from falling backward.

Mr. Tobin made big scooping motions with his arms. "Come on, Amelia Bedelia!" he hollered. "Fall toward me."

She leaned forward and hit the sand.

"I've never been so happy to fall on my face," she said as Mr. Tobin measured her jump and the crowd cheered.

"Congratulations," he said. "Your jump put you in first place!"

"Amelia Bedelia!" shouted Coach. "Great jump! Sorry about the whistle! We had a situation."

Amelia Bedelia waved and smiled. She felt funny in first, after being second so many times. She didn't get to feel funny for long. Skip bested her best by two inches, just the length of one of her mother's yummy brownies! So Amelia Bedelia came in second for the fourth time in a row.

The real surprise came in the fifth and final event—wrestling. Who knew that Amelia Bedelia would be such a star? She won match after match! The final match of the

pentathlon pitted her against her friend Angel, who was the sweetest and kindest person she knew. Amelia Bedelia was almost positive she would beat Angel.

She didn't want to, but if she pretended they were ancient Greek girls, it wouldn't be so bad. She wished Angel good luck and planted her feet.

"Thanks," said Angel. "I hope you win, Amelia Bedelia."

Coach blew her whistle to start the final match. In seconds, Angel was all over Amelia Bedelia. Slipping behind her in a flash, Angel wrapped her arms around Amelia Bedelia, pinning both of Amelia Bedelia's arms while using a leg to sweep her off her feet. BOOM! Down went Amelia Bedelia, with Angel on top.

TWEET!

Coach raised Angel's arm in triumph. The match was over! Already?

"Wow!" said Amelia Bedelia. "That was amazing!" She gave Angel a high penta and a hug.

Amelia Bedelia was second again!

Chapter 14

When Second Comes First

Mr. Tobin thanked everyone for participating in the Greek Games—the students for their enthusiasm, and the parents and other teachers for their support, especially Coach Thompson, who got a big round of applause.

Mr. Tobin went on, "As my good friend Aristotle said, 'A body capable of enduring

all efforts, either of the racecourse or of bodily strength . . . is why the athletes in the pentathlon are most beautiful.' Thank you all for making this such a beautiful and fun day at our school."

Parents clapped loudly, and the students cheered.

"Our winners today will be awarded the highest honor in ancient Greece, a wreath of laurel leaves to wear on their heads as a symbol of their victory."

Mr. Tobin and Coach stood at the front, holding six wreaths.

Five events = five winners, which does not = six wreaths, thought Amelia Bedelia.

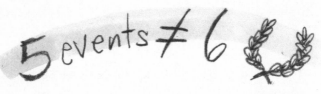

These Greek Games were not adding up.

Mr. Tobin called the winners to come forward. He announced the winners' names, the events they had won, and their winning time or distance. Then Coach placed a wreath on each winner's head, and they all shook hands. When the fifth one had been presented, Mr. Tobin held up one last wreath.

"This is an extra wreath," he said. "It was made by mistake, but now I think it was not a mistake at all. One athlete among you never knew the thrill of coming in first. Second place was as close as she came. But that student did it five times. Let me tell you, being in second place five times adds up to being the best all-around athlete in our class. Where is Amelia Bedelia?"

Amelia Bedelia had been in the back, but now a path cleared for her to come forward. Mr. Tobin handed the wreath to Coach, who placed it on Amelia Bedelia's head. Then she said, "You worked hard to make yourself stronger and faster. Even though you didn't win any events, you always cheered your classmates on. You

5 × 2nd = Best All-Around

captured the spirit of good sportsmanship, born in ancient Greece, and helped make these Greek Games a success."

Everyone was clapping loudly, cheering and stomping their feet.

"I declare these Greek Games over," said Mr. Tobin. "Let's eat!"

Everyone enjoyed a picnic lunch on colorful blankets on the grass where minutes before they had been throwing, racing, tossing, jumping, and wrestling. Mr. Tobin and Coach came by to thank Amelia Bedelia's mother for her delicious honey cake.

"We both took huge slices," said Coach.

"Yes," said Mr. Tobin. "We put a dent in it."

"It was dented from the start," said Amelia Bedelia's mother.

"Put your laurel wreath back on, sweetie," said Amelia Bedelia's father. "I want to get a picture of you with Mr. Tobin and Coach Thompson."

Amelia Bedelia touched the top of her head, but her wreath was gone. How could she have lost it, after all she went through to win it?

"There it is," said her mother. "You're sitting on it."

"Aha!" said Mr. Tobin. "Are you resting on your laurels already, Amelia Bedelia?"

She put her wreath back on her head, and her dad took a picture that ended up in the school newspaper.

On their way home, Amelia Bedelia's father leaned over and said to his wife,

"Honey, at our next parent meeting with Mr. Tobin, remind me to suggest a celebration of golf. I could volunteer and show the kids how to putt and—"

"Drive golf carts?" asked Amelia Bedelia.

"Not your father," said Amelia Bedelia's mother. "He only golfs for the exercise."

Amelia Bedelia and her dad winked at each other in the rearview mirror.

"I know we just came from a picnic," he said. "But I could use a bite to eat right now."

"Me too," said Amelia Bedelia. "I'm starving after all that exercise."

Amelia Bedelia's mother made a suggestion. "We could get french fries at Pete's Diner."

"Pete's is nice," said Amelia Bedelia's father. "But I was hoping to work on my slice."

Amelia Bedelia's mother shook her head. "Golf!" she said. "Is golf the only thing you think about?"

"Of course not," said Amelia Bedelia's father. "I was thinking that we could go to Perfect Pizza, and then I'll work on a slice with pepperoni and a slice with sausage and a slice with extra cheese." And that is exactly what they did.

Two Ways to Say It

By Amelia Bedelia

"I'm bringing home the bacon."

"I'm providing for my family."

"It's time to hit the sack."

"It's time to go to bed."

"I'd rather watch paint dry."

"I'd rather do anything else."

"Her ears were burning."

"Someone was talking about her."

"He's snug as a bug."

"He's very comfortable."

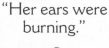

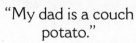

"My dad is a couch potato."

"My dad likes to sit around relaxing."

"You are a good sport."

"You are fair and agreeable."

"She won by a nose."

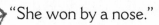

"She barely beat the other person."

"Don't rest on your laurels!"

"Keep trying and working hard, even though you've already done so many great things!"

"Stand tall!"

"Be strong and proud of yourself!"

Coming soon!

Amelia Bedelia

Hi!
Turn the page
for a special
sneak peek
at my next
adventure!

Chapter 1

Breezy? Yes. Easy? No . . .

Amelia Bedelia was as free as a bird. She was pedaling her bike as fast as she could. The wind was blowing in her face and blowing her hair straight back. Now she understood why Finally, her dog, loved to hang her head out the car window on trips. Amelia Bedelia really wished that every day was this easy and breezy.

Today she was riding all over town with her friends Holly and Heather. They zipped through the park, zooming by babies in strollers, and woofing at the dogs out for a walk. The dogs woofed right back.

"Let's go this way!" shouted Holly.

"Follow me!" yelled Heather.

Amelia Bedelia raced behind her friends. As she pedaled, she imagined changing her name officially. Then people would call out, "There goes Amelia Breezelia, Club President!"

The Amelia Bedelia Chapter Books
Have you read them all?

Coming
Soon!

Coming
Soon!